MAYOR GOOD BOY

ALSO BY DAVE SCHEIDT

Wrapped Up

MAYOR GOOD BOY

Written by Dave Scheidt
Illustrated by Miranda Harmon

ZOO

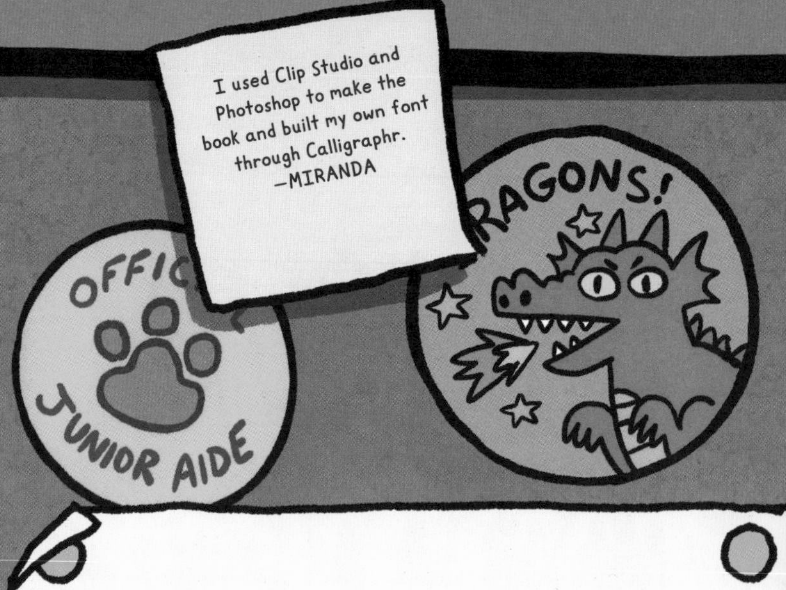
I used Clip Studio and Photoshop to make the book and built my own font through Calligraphr.
—MIRANDA
OFFIC
JUNIOR AIDE
RAGONS!

This is a work of fiction. Names, characters, places, and incidents either are the product of the author's imagination or are used fictitiously. Any resemblance to actual persons, living or dead, events, or locales is entirely coincidental.

 Published in the United States by RH Graphic, an imprint of Random House Children's Books, a division of Penguin Random House LLC, New York.

RH Graphic with the book design is a trademark of Penguin Random House LLC.

Visit us on the web! RHKidsGraphic.com • @RHKidsGraphic

Educators and librarians, for a variety of teaching tools, visit us at RHTeachersLibrarians.com

Library of Congress Cataloging-in-Publication Data is available upon request.
ISBN 978-0-593-12487-1 (hardcover) — ISBN 978-0-593-12537-3 (library binding)
ISBN 978-0-593-12488-8 (ebook)

Designed by Patrick Crotty

MANUFACTURED IN CHINA
10 9 8 7 6 5 4 3 2 1
First Edition

RH
GRAPHIC

A comic on every bookshelf.

ABBY ABLEMAN
2nd Place Science Fair
FOR NATALIE
—D.S.
FOR MOM AND DAD.
THANK YOU FOR ALL
YOUR LOVE.
—M.H.
Nice Slice with the gang! 4/14

Good evening, Greenwood!
GREENWOOD
CITY HALL

We're here outside city hall, just minutes away from finding out who our next mayor is!
MAYOR GOOD BOY
BE GOOD, GREEN-WOOD!

What a cute little family!

What's your name, little boy?
BUUURP

This weirdo is my little brother, Aaron.
And what's your name?

Uhh. My name is Abby...
Huh?

We have some breaking news! The results are in!

Please, please, please...

Dad. Quick. Give me your phone!

Abby! You want to take some weird selfies? Watch this!
Hang on! Something is happening!

The results are in, and boy oh boy, are things about to get weird in Greenwood!

What are they saying?
Who won? It better not be who I think it is!

People of Greenwood! Your new mayor is...

MAYOR GOOD BOY!!
WOOO-HOOO!

Wow. I can't believe he won.
YESSS!!

I'm not going to let some mangy mutt ruin our town!
What's next? We pick a BEETLE as our senator?
Aww! I love bugs!

Can't be any worse than our last mayor!
He smelled like old candy and armpits!
WOW

I say we go have a talk with this new mayor of ours and tell him how we feel!
Yeah!

CITY HALL
Uh-oh.

That's right, folks.
The votes are in, and the new mayor of Greenwood is a dog!
We're about to hear Good Boy make his first speech as mayor.

What now?
Should we... do something?

Well, what are you waiting for? Go!
CITY HALL

Okay, so this is happening, I guess?

It is my honor to introduce to you my dear friend Mayor Good Boy!

He's even fluffier in real life!
Woo!

Psst, Ms. Monica!
I don't think I can do this!

Get. Out. Here.

We're having a little technical problem. One second, everyone!

YAWN

I'm freaking out, man! I thought I was ready to do this, but now I feel like I'm gonna barf!

I knew you were going to do this.

SNIFF SNIFF
Is that...

CHEESE!

ZOOOOOM

MUNCH
MUNCH
WOOOO!
YEAH!

Oh. Hey!

ahem

GRUNT

Nice and easy!

Wait.
That's not right.

WOBBLE
WOBBLE

Okay.
Where was I?
You haven't
said anything yet!

What's up,
Greenwood?

EXIT
BOOM
BOOM

Uhh, come in?

EXIT

Greenwood can't be run by a DOG!
Yeah, what's next? We hire a PIG as a CHEF?
Aww! Piggy chef!

Chill out!
Everything is cool!
Okay?

SPLAT
Did you just
throw a papaya?
That's a weird
choice.

You're one to
talk about weird
choices!
Let's
get 'em!

Hey. Maybe we should get out of here. This doesn't seem safe.

I think it's fine. People are just excited!

SPLAT
WATERMELON!

KAPOW
Okay! Time to go!
KRAK
WHAM

What are we going to do?

THERE HE IS!
Nowhere to run now, little doggie!

Aaron, I can't believe I'm saying this, but can you take off your shoes?
SURE!

FWIP

Now what?

UGH, what's that smell?
It smells like my pep-pep's barn!
It smells like a zombie's gym towel!

Aaron, do me a favor and stand in front of that fan over there.

Man. What is that smell? GROSS!
I'm gonna barf.

HA HA HA
HA HA HA

I'm gonna be sick!
EXIT
Need...air...

You really saved my tail! If it weren't for your stinky socks, I would have been in big trouble!
MAYOR

Ew. What? No! Those were my brother Aaron's socks.
It was kind of my idea, though...

Thank you for your service, Aaron. Your gross feet are the kind of heroes this town needs.
My pleasure!

Abby! I could really use a big smart brain like yours around town!

Ehh, I dunno...
I'm not sure I could
be much help...

Oh, that is
SUCH a good idea,
Ms. Monica!
whisper
whisper

Excuse me for
a second.
YAAAWN

Umm?
zzzzz

ZZZZZZ-

BORK
BORK BORK

Aren't you forgetting something, Mr. Mayor?
Yeah. Aren't you going to offer us any cheese?

Didn't you have something to ask Abby and Aaron?
HA HA HA
Oh yeah!

You guys want a job?
MAYOR
GOOD

Abby and Aaron's house.
The next morning.

JAWS

THUD
ABBY, WAKE UP!
ABBY! ABBY!

I'M AWAKE!
I'M AWAKE!

Check out my sick outfit!
Aaron, you look like a grown man who was turned into a kid by a witch.

You know what, Abby? I'll take that as a compliment 'cause witches are COOL.

Why did you wake me up so early? We don't have to meet with the mayor for another three hours!

I couldn't sleep! We're getting JOBS, Abby. That means we're grown-ups now.
Maybe Mayor Good Boy will give us a baby to take care of.

Aaron, what are you talking about? Why would he give us a baby?
Dad told me that the most important job in the world is raising a baby.

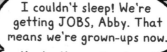

I don't think that's the job he wants us to do, Aaron.
KLINK
KLINK

I guess we'll see. I love babies. They're cute.

SNIFF
SNIFF

PANCAKES!

SSSSSIZZLE

PANCAKES!
MY FAVORITE!

That my old tuxedo?
Looking good, my man!
Thanks!
Tell that to
Abby.

Coming at ya!
FLIP

NAILED IT!

Whoa, Abby. You get any sleep last night?
No. Not really. I was up the whole night thinking about all the ways I could mess up today.

Oh, Abby. You're too hard on yourself. I think you're great.

So today is the big day, huh? My little Abby and Aaron...

Dad, please don't...

I am so proud of you kids. You are just like your mother. Smart and beautiful.
...cry.

You two are going
to do great things. I am
so happy to be your dad.

You're...
choking...
me...

Love you
too, Dad.

Aaron! We gotta go!
I want to grab a few
things before our
first day.

Later, skaters!

I'm SO nervous. I feel like I'm gonna barf!
Please don't barf on my tux.

Seriously, though. You got this! Just act casual!

Morning, Abby! Morning, Aaron!
Good morning, Mr. Kupperman!

Morning, Ms. Stanley! Morning, Admiral Meowington!
MROW!

Ching's Bakery
I'm going to bribe Mayor Good Boy with treats so he'll love us!
Open
Dad is right. You're pretty AND smart.

I'm not buying you anything.

Worth a shot.

Hi, Mr. Ching!
ABBY! AARON! WHAT A NICE SURPRISE!

Want to try our brand-new top secret cookies?
Milk Tea 1.25
Latte 2.00
Uh, YES?
YES, PLEASE!

MMMmmm, these are so good!
I wish I could eat these cookies until I died. It would be worth it.

They are good, right? I think these are going to be a big hit! I keep the recipe hidden safely away so nobody copies me!

Hey, do you have any fancy cheese? I wanted to get some for my new boss.

Are you kidding me? I got the best cheese in town! Who is your boss?

Mayor Good Boy.

Did you say MAYOR GOOD BOY?

I'm one of his biggest supporters! Gimme one second!
BE GOOD
GREENWOOD

Please send my love to the mayor.

Also make sure Ms. Monica gets this. I think she's...cool...but, like, not in a weird way or anything....
A sweet treat for a sweet lady

I really hope Mayor Good Boy likes this stuff...
GREENWOOD THEATER
25th ANNUAL SPOOKATHON
I hope he wants to be friends with us!
FLOWERS
Rewind Records
Yeah, right. Who would want to be friends with a weirdo like me?
CITY HALL
There it is! Don't freak out... Don't freak out...
Whoa! Look! ALIENS!

Step away, children!
We're disposing of some very dangerous toxic material!

Are you guys ALIENS? Can I hold your death ray? Do you want to come over for dinner?

OH NO!
HA HA
HA
SLIIIP

PLEASE, NOOOOOO!

GET IT OFF! GET IT OFF!

Hang in there, man!

FWIIIIT

CLICK

WHOOOSH

THAT WAS THE COOLEST THING I HAVE EVER SEEN IN MY ENTIRE LIFE! ALIENS JUST DESTROYED MY STINKY SOCKS!
CLAP CLAP

Thank you, aliens! It was great meeting you!
C'mon, Aaron. We gotta go!

PAT PAT PAT PAT

Yeah. I can't do this. Bye!
Heads up!
ZZZZZZ

You made it!

Hi, Ms. Monica, I'm not sure if you remember me but—
ABBY! AARON!

I wanted to thank you. If it weren't for you two, I don't know what would have happened!
You probably would have died.

HA HA HA! I'm glad we didn't die. That wouldn't have been cool.

Look at you, Aaron! You are KILLING it with that tuxedo!

Told ya!

I love your leather jacket! I have one just like it! We should start a girl gang!

That would be...cool.

Follow me! I'll show you to Mayor Good Boy's office. He's so excited you're here.

Okay, Abby, you got this.

Mayor
You guys ready?

Stand still.
PAT
PAT

WIPE
WIPE

Yeah. Okay.
Now we're ready!

We, uh...
We brought
you some...
ZZZZZZZZZ
M. GOOD BOY

Cheese?
THUD

BORK
BORK

BORK
BORK
BORK
BORK
BORK

ahem
Excuse me!

WHOOOSH

Abby! Aaron!
Please sit down.

NOM NOM NOM

AHEM

Oh, forgive me! Would you guys like some of this cheese?

No thanks.

MMMM cheese!
SLAP

GREENWOOD
First of all, thank you SO much for being here!

There is something about you kids... You got something special!

Aww...

What do you mean, "special"? Like if I was born with TWO butts instead of ONE?

Whoa! TWO butts? Now, THAT would be something special!

Here's a list of things we need your help taking care of around town. I think you guys will be able to smooth things over with all our constituents.

HA
HA HA
HA HA
HA HA
HA

Constituents are all the people in town that I promised to protect and take care of! That we're going to take care of together!

You can count on us, Mayor Good Boy!

I hope...

Okay. It looks like there's something going on at the zoo today!
•Zoo
•Community garden
•Summer Camp?
•Water park?
•Free pizza!
•Movie theater
•Food trucks
•Little libraries
•Anti-Good Boy Society
•Bad Boy

I love the zoo! Let's go!
Plus, they have chicken nuggets.

Let's do it!

Let me just text Ms. Monica...

M. Monica
Hey Ms. Monica!! It's Abby. we're headed to the zoo! What are we supposed to do?

AARON, SHE'S RESPONDING! I can't believe I have a real live texting friend now!

SSSIP
Ms. Monica

M. Monica
No way! That's so great to hear! I'm going to wake the mayor up from his seventh nap and we'll come meet ya!

Mayor Good Boy and Ms. Monica are going to come meet us. We can't mess this up.

This is gonna be awesome!

Almost...there...

Abby, slow down so I can die.

ZOO
Sigh. We *huff* made *huff* it.

YO!

Nice to see you again!

You look like those guys from that movie who get eaten by dinosaurs!
Uh, thanks?

We got you uniforms too! Check it out!

YESSSS!
Maybe a T. rex will eat us now, and then I won't have to go back to school!

This shirt fits weird!

Ha ha ha, those are shorts, Aaron.

I knew that was a test! I wanted to see if you would say something. Good job.

Man, you guys look so cool! You ready for this?

This event is a sort of meet and greet called Getting Wild with the Mayor.

We think it'll be a great opportunity for the people of Greenwood to meet Mayor Good Boy while helping the zoo raise some money.

Aww! That is such a good idea! How can we help?

Here's a sign-in sheet. Make sure everyone who shows up signs this!

Oh, and keep an eye out for this weirdo.

You may have seen this grump on election night. He's declared Mayor Good Boy his mortal enemy.
Aren't old people supposed to be kind and smart and give you gross candy?

Not this guy. His name is Mervis Hogpepper. He's started a group called the Anti-Good Boy Society, and he's trying to recruit as many people as possible.
He thinks Mayor Good Boy is going to ruin Greenwood.
SIPPP

So what do you want us to do? Kill him or something?
SPFFFF

That's nice of you to offer your services, Aaron, but that's very illegal.

Just keep an eye out for him. If you see him, let me know.

Look! People are starting to show up!

Mayor Good Boy! You are awfully quiet. Is everything okay?

Of course.
ZZZZZZZZZ

If anyone would like to make any donations to the Mayor Good Boy snack fund, please see me.

Hahaha, that is so funny!
Such cute kids!
What a funny joke!

I would NEVER joke about snacks. That's the only thing in life I will ever take seriously.

CLAP
CLAP
ZZZZZZZ

?? !
Huh?
What? Huh?

How was your nap?

Oh yeah. Pretty good! I could have used like eleven more hours, but this will do!

Back to business!

Wow! What a turnout!
Yeah, there must be like... a million people here.
Twenty-seven people, actually.
027
GRRRROWL
RESTROOM
Hey, Abby. I'm going to go use the bathroom real quick.
You need me to come with you?
I'm not a baby. It's right there.
Come right back, okay? We still need to keep an eye out for that weird old guy.
Yeah, yeah.

SNACKS
FOOD
DRINK
There we go.

Can I have a six-piece chicken nuggets? I don't need a bag. The less evidence, the better...
FOOD
JUNGLE BURG
DINO NUGGETS
CHEETAH CHILI
RINKS
LEPHANT WATER
LAR SLUSH

Hey, you haven't seen any scary old men around here, have you?
That's like eighty percent of our visitors. Have a nice day.

THE MAYOR
Sorry, we need to take another one. My teeth looked weird.

THE
We look SO cute!
Wow, we DO look cute!
MAYOR GOOD BOY
Next!

Hey, buddy! So good to meet you.
Hi...
MAYOR GOOD BOY

Do...do you... want to sign my cast?

I can't believe Mayor Good Boy is signing my cast!

Thank you so much. No one at school wanted to sign it, but just wait till they see who did!

Man. Where is Aaron? He should have been back by now.

Abby, is everything okay?

Yeah, I think Aaron is just getting into trouble somewhere. I'll be right back.

Text me!
Okay!

♫Chicken ♪ nuggets!
♪ Chicken ♪ nuggets!
SNIFF SNIFF
OOOOOOOOOOH
YOINK!

Ooo
OOO
Ooo!

Those are MY nuggets, you jerk!

Heh! Not anymore!

Well, I guess that's karma.

CLICK

Aaron?
Aaron?

Someone do something!
GET OUT, KID! IT AIN'T SAFE!

Found him.

Excuse me! Pardon me! Big sister coming through!

SHAKE
SHAKE
Ugh, so hungry!
GRRROWL
OOOK
OOOK
Why don't you just buy more chicken nuggets?
Dude, I'm eight! I don't have any money!
Plus, stealing is wrong!
I'm coming for ya!

AARON ABLEMAN! GET DOWN HERE RIGHT NOW!

Oh, hey, Abby! I'll be right out. Let me just grab my nuggets.

That's your little brother?
Unfortunately.

Wait till Mom and Dad hear about this!

Okay! Fine!

Coming down!

MUNCH MUNCH MUNCH

This isn't over! You hear me?

OOK OOK OOK

How did you even get in there? We're supposed to be helping Mayor Good Boy!
I stole the keys from some mean guy with a ponytail!
JINGLE
JINGLE
See? Nothing bad even happened!
YOINK
OOK OOK
Okay, I didn't see that one coming.

OOK OOK OOK OOK
OOK OOK OOK
OOK
OOK OOK

Oh no!
He's freeing the
other animals,
too!
Oh no! What
if they eat all the
snacks in the zoo?
What then?

We gotta
go warn Mayor
Good Boy!

RUNNN!
WE HAVE TO SAVE
THE SNACKS!

Aww, look at those wittle bitty cheeks!
MAYOR GOOD BOY

So... sleepy...

Hey! Watch where you're going!
Outta the way!

Surprised to see me?

Nice little crowd you have here today. It would be a shame if they found out the truth!
MAYOR GOOD BOY

And what truth would that be, Mervis?

That little fleabag next to you isn't fit to run our town!
LEASH THE MUTT

Hey! I haven't had fleas since I was a puppy!

Let's all try to chill out a bit, okay?

Aaron. Whatever you do, don't look back.

MEET THE

RUN!
That koala stole my churro!

Good crocky...

Go, sloth, go!

...AND
ANOTHER THING!
HUH?

MAYOR GOOD
BOY! LOOK OUT!
IT'S THAT GUY!

Can you keep
it down, please?
I'm trying
to yell.

MAYOR GOOD BOY, WE HAVE TO GO. AARON
BOUGHT CHICKEN NUGGETS BUT AN APE
STOLE THEM AND AARON SNUCK INTO THE CAGE
AND THE APE ESCAPED AND LET OUT
ALL THE OTHER
ANIMALS!

WAIT A SECOND. ARE YOU SERIOUS?

They have chicken nuggets here?

AAAAAPE!

GET IT OFF ME!
GET IT OFF ME!

Ahhhhh!
GET OFF!

RUMBLE RUMBLE

We've got company.

What are we gonna do?
I can't die! Think of all th snacks I'll never try!

Mayor Good Boy, what do we do?
They are getting closer!

• • •

Okay. Step aside. I'll handle this.

Mayor Good Boy! Wait! You'll get hurt!

Don't worry, kids. He always finds a way. It's kind of his thing.

I hope he knows what he's doing.

BORK
BORK
BORK
BORK
BORK
BORK

BORK
BORK
BORK

BORK
BORK
BORK
BORK
BORK
BORK

BORK

MEET THE MAYO
Whoa.

That. Was. AWESOME!
All bork. No bite. Sometimes that's all it takes!
Sorry I ruined everything, Mayor Good Boy...
It's okay, Aaron. We can talk about it tomorrow.
I forgive you. You just owe me some chicken nuggets next time.
HAHAHA, EW, GROSS! GET OFF!
HA HA
HA
HA
HA
HA

We're outside Greenwood Zoo, where less than twelve hours ago, a young boy's gluttonous mistake descended the zoo into utter chaos and released a pack of wild animals upon the citizens of Greenwood.
ZOO
Steenz Stewart
Monkey Business in Greenwood!

I could see it in his eyes, man. That ape is LUCKY that kid didn't catch him.
The second that chimp yanked that kid's chicken nuggets, darkness filled his eyes.

Did you see what he looked like?

He looked exactly like this.

Thankfully almost all the animals were apprehended last night besides one.

Please be advised that this ape is still on the loose and considered unarmed and extremely into chicken nuggets.

Well, I guess it could have been worse?
CLICK

I guess I don't need my disguise anymore, then? NICE!

You think that just because you got away with it last night makes it okay?

No...
but...

You could
have gotten yourself
hurt or worse!

That was a
really bad idea,
Aaron.
I'm
sorry...

Look, man. I get it.
Chicken nuggets are great.
They are probably in my top
five, but you CANNOT
do stuff like that
anymore, okay?

Did you see that chimp crawling on Old Man Mervis?

"GET IT OFF! GET IT OFF!"

HA HA HA HA HA HA HA HA HA HA HA

That was almost worth it.

Almost.

I am really, really sorry we let you down, Mayor Good Boy.
I hope we can make it up to you.

I got another job for you guys!

Oh! Oh! Is it a spy mission?

Special Agent Aaron Ableman reporting for duty.

It's actually cooler than that! It's...

YARDWORK? GROSS!

You got it! We want to turn this into a community garden! Maybe organize a farmers market?
SNIFF SNIFF

DUDE, WE CAN MAKE FRESH GUACAMOLE!

Awww, and maybe plant a cute little rosebush?
Oh my gosh, that would be so pretty!

This is fun for you guys? What planet are you from?

This isn't about us, Aaron. It's about Greenwood. We're doing this for the community.
Hmphh.

Hard work pays off. Trust me. You'll see.

Okay. I trust you.

SNIFF
SNIFF

AACHOooo
!

A few hours later...
See!
Look at that!
A real community garden.
What a lightweight!
ZZZZZZ
You guys did an amazing job today. Thank you.
No.
Thank you.

BEEP
BEEP

Sounds like my parents are here!

Hi, Mr. Mayor!

SKIP SKIP
SKIP
ZZZZZ

ZZZZZ

Ahem

Okay.
Come on.

I just wanted to let you know that you have some really great kids.

Aww, thank you. That means a lot.

They really need someone like you around.

I don't think I've ever seen them this quiet before.

Just like old times, huh?
Sure is.

GROSS!

Aaron, you are literally the grossest kid on this planet.
HA HA HA HA
HA HA
HA
HA
Thank you. I'll take that as a compliment.

Put him on a leash!
Do we REALLY want
a DOG as a mayor?
Join the Anti-Good
Boy Society and
take Greenwood
back!

This is a town for PEOPLE! Who wants to have a DOG in charge?

Yeah!
SEND HIM BACK TO THE POUND, WHERE HE BELONGS!

A chimp tried to peel my head like a coconut!
And it was ALL Mayor Good Boy's fault!

HA HA
HA HA

Something funny, liver lips?

Sorry... I thought that was a joke. The chimp attack thing?

Does THIS look funny to you?

I'm sorry... It's just...A CHIMP WAS ON TOP OF YOUR HEAD! THAT IS SO FUNNY!

HA HA
HA HEE
HEE
HA HEE HEE
HA HA
HA

Let's get something straight here. The next person who laughs at me will wish they were never born!

You think what happened at the zoo was bad? This is only the beginning! It's up to us to take back Greenwood!

Yeah! He's right!
What's next? A cat that plays heavy metal?
AWW! Metal kitty!

I need you knocking on every door in Greenwood to let everyone know that Good Boy's gotta go!

HEY HO! HEY HO!
GOOD BOY'S GOTTA GO!

Mayor Good Boy? We have a little problem...
HEY HO! HEY HO! GOOD BOY'S GOTTA GO!

RecOrds
Dandelion Café
MOVIES
106

I've seen a lot of mayors come and go here in Greenwood...
GOOD BOY ACTUALLY BAD?

And let me tell you, this town has never been this exciting!

He's so polite too! He was here last week and couldn't have been nicer. He was the only one who noticed my new haircut!

Have you seen this? I've been seeing them all over town lately!

SEND HIM
BACK TO THE
POUND!

Boutique
Chuck's
Meats

RRIPP

ZZZZZZZZZ

12 p.m.
Mayor

RING RING RINGGG

Mayor Good Boy's office! This is Abby speaking! How can I help you?

I have a question.

I'd love to help!

Can you send that mutt back to the pound?
CLICK

Ugh! That is like the seventh prank phone call today!
Next time hand me the phone.

What are you going to say that I can't?
I'm not going to say anything...

I'll just fart into the phone. Like this.

You're disgusting. I'm not going to let you fart into the phone.

Let me answer it!
Just don't fart or burp or do anything gross, okay?
RING
RING
RING

Asking me not to be gross is like asking Dad not to be embarrassing. It's not going to happen.
Just answer the phone, Aaron.

Yeah? What do you want?

I mean... Mayor Good Boy's office. This is Aaron. How can I help you?

Help! Bigfoot keeps breaking into my house and trying on my underwear! He also hacked my Wi-Fi and tried to steal my credit card number!

Who tries to order ten boxes of beef jerky and trail mix? BIGFOOT! That's who!
Psst, Abby.

Is it the Bigfoot guy again? Just tell him we'll send someone out.

We'll send someone out soon, sir.
Can you deal with the aliens, too? Their technology is disrupting my microwave frequencies and not cooking my TV dinners right.
Yes. Of course we'll take care of the aliens, too. See you soon.

How often does that guy call?
CLICK

CRUNCH CRUNCH
Every. Single. Day.

You guys are doing great, by the way. I'm able to get so much work done having you around.
It's been fun. You never know what sort of person is going to call next!
ARE THOSE CHIPS?
RUSTLE RUSTLE
MUNCH MUNCH
RUSTLE RUSTLE
I'll grab this one.
RING RING
Okay. Okay. We'll be right there, ma'am.
We got work to do! Let's do it.

Minutes later...
Oh my goodness! Thank you for coming!
So what's going on here?
These raccoons keep eating through our roof! I tried to scare them away, but they just climbed up this tree.
chit chit Chit Chittt
That's not even the end of it! My grandson spots the raccoons and climbs up the tree and tries to play with them, and now he's stuck up there too!
Yo.

Don't worry, little guy! We'll get you down soon! Hold on tight!

Whoa! Is that Mayor Good Boy?
Would it be rude if I pet him?

No need to worry, ma'am. I have a very talented group of friends with me who can help.

I'm too old to try to climb up one of those trees! My husband broke his bottom in the war, so he's no help, either!
Took a grenade to the butt in '68! It's 95% stainless steel now!

What's going on?
Some little kid is stuck in a tree, and that old guy has a fake butt!

You're looking at the best tree climber in the neighborhood!
It's true!

I have a plan! Mayor Good Boy, I can get you up there. I just need you to hold on tight!

Hop on my shoulder!

BOIIING

Oooof.
You are a big
boy, aren't you?
I eat a lot
of cheese.
Dude.
Same.

Be careful,
you guys!

Look
at him go!

Ughhh,
so close...

This branch looks nice and strong. I'm gonna let you down, okay?
Okay. Don't drop me!

See? No problemo.

HISSSSSSSSSSSS

You take care of those raccoons, and I'll take care of that kid!
What if I don't want to come down?
Sorry, little bro. Party's over.

PSSH

WOBBLE
WOBBLE

What's your problem, man? I'm just up here trying to kick it with my bros.
Yeah!

Hey. I feel you. I just think maybe it would be better to find somewhere else to chill.
That old lady threw a shoe at me! Very disrespectful.

It's bad enough that we got that weird kid always trying to hug us! It's like...back off, kid! I don't know you like that!

Wait a second...Mayor Good Boy can speak raccoon?
VEG FEST 2016

Ha! I guess so!

Wow. Is there anything Mayor Good Boy can't do?
VEG FEST 2016

Dogs can't eat chocolate. They'll die.
VEG FEST 2016

Respect.
VEG FEST 2016

I'll tell you what. How would you guys like a job? It'll give you somewhere else to go.

Please tell me more.

(whisper whisper)

That sounds tight. See you soon! Let's roll out, fellas.

Hey! Where are you going? I still need to hug you!

SHAKE
SHAKE

HUG ME!

UH-OH!

MAYOR GOOD BOY, PLEASE SAVE MY GRANDSON!

CRACK!

Hang on...
RIPPP

I'm going to pull you up, okay?
sob Okay!

Got you! Nice and easy!

Mayor Good Boy and that brave little boy are heroes!
Yeah!
Woo-hoo!

That's my little brother!

Hang on tight, okay?
We're almost there.

You saved him!

I was worried sick about you! Please don't ever do something like that again, okay?
SQUEEEEZE
Sorry, Grandma...

And you! My grandson could have gotten really hurt if it wasn't for you and the mayor!

I'm going to tell everyone in town about how great you and your big sister and Mayor Good Boy are! You are the kind of leaders Greenwood needs the most!
SQUEEEEZE

I feel like we're forgetting something.

Uh, hello? Little help?

Jump down! We got you!

We'll catch you, Mr. Mayor!
Trust us!
GREENWOOD'S GOT YOU!

Okay, Good Boy. You got this, dude!

HERE WE...

GO!

WOO-HOOOOO!

GOOD BOY! GOOD BO
OOD BOY! GOOD BOY!

Yuck!
Cheering for a
mangy ol' MUTT!
REEEEAL
NICE!

What's your
problem?
Outta
the way, you
dingbats!
Watch it!

Hey!

DON'T "HEY" ME!
You got a lot of nerve
showing your tail
around here!

MAYOR
GOOD BOY,
LOOK OUT!

QUIET!
An adult is
talking!

Aww!
Did I hurt your
little feelings?
CRUNCHHH

BORK
BORK
BORK

Everyone
just chill out,
okay?

This beautiful,
stunning silky angel
boy right here is
a HERO!

In case you forgot, this little cutie is the MAYOR! You're lucky he doesn't kick you out of town!

YEAH!
TAKE A HIKE!

If it weren't for Mayor Good Boy and these kids, my grandson could have gotten hurt!

You leave the mayor alone, or you'll have to deal with me!

I'm going to leave because I feel like leaving! Not because you told me to!

You'll regret this! Just you wait! That little mutt is gonna destroy Greenwood!

See ya!
Never come back! Byeeee!

Mayor Good Boy! What's wrong?
I don't trust that guy.

Be ready to start the plan! Greenwood is about to get interesting...

The next morning. 3:16 a.m.
GREENWOOD EXTERMINATORS

So they want to hand over our town to the dogs, huh?

Let's see how they enjoy living like dogs!
ZZZZIP

HEH HEH HEH
GREENWOOD EXTERMINATORS

FLEA
VACUUM

FLEA
VACUUM
EXHAUST
INTAKE

GREENWOOD
EXTERMINATORS

All set, boss?

It's about to get a little itchy in Greenwood. Ha ha ha ha!
FLEA
VACUUM

GREENWOOD
EXTERMINATORS

Releasing the fleas!
EXHAUST

VROOOM

Ha ha ha! This is all your fault, Greenwood! Hope you're happy.
GREENWOOD
EXTERMINATORS

BOING
BOING
BOING
Sarah's Dry Cleaning
BOX OFFICE
CLOSED
READ!
Fleas
Fleas
More fleas
Fleas
CITY HALL
So many fleas
Fleas

We're in a MASSIVE flea infestation...
Excuse me a second.

So itchy...

Greenwood is covered in fleas...
I CAN'T DO THIS!

WOMP

I'M SO ITCHY!

Wow. This is bad. Thank goodness I flea-proofed this place already!

What do you think is going on?

I don't know, but it's not good!

The phone won't stop ringing! People are afraid to leave their houses!
This flea infestation is all over town!

This is horrible! What are we going to do?
Oh yeah! There we go.

SHOO!
SHOO!
POPCOR

Uh-oh.

SCRATCH
SCRATCH
SCRATCH
SCRATCH

Fleas aren't THAT big of a deal! I got lice one time in kindergarten and I didn't have to go to school for a week! Best thing that has ever happened to me.

It IS a big deal. People are going to think this is Mayor Good Boy's fault!

It's true. We need to get out there and help.

We can't go outside like this.

It's time to gear up!

Man! I can't believe Mayor Good Boy has an arsenal!

Uhh, sure. I guess you could call it that?
CLICK

Gear! Gear! Gear!

Huh?

What the heck is all this?
GOOD BOY

Where are all your flamethrowers? Bazookas? Samurai swords?
GOOD BOY

Aaron... What exactly do you think the mayor does? Why would we need a flamethrower?

Cachooooo Goodbye, fleas! Just like that Aliens movie!

Wow. I mean, that actually WOULD come in handy, but no, Aaron. Mayors' offices usually don't have a flamethrower.

PAT PAT PAT

Here.
Put these on.

Why do you want us to wear dog collars?

Oh my gosh! Mayor Good Boy! You're so smart!

These are flea collars! They're like anti-flea force fields!

We're gonna look so cool!

HMMM?

Why are these so hard to put on? Man.

Why is Aaron like this?
I ask myself that every day...

So what's the plan?

The plan is to get enough of these collars to everyone in town while we try to get an exterminator out here.

It's weird 'cause the town exterminator isn't answering his phone. Like the one time we really need him!

Wow.
That is weird...

We have a bigger storage locker right here. There's a HUGE surplus of flea collars from the election inside here that we can pass out around town!
GREENWOOD
MALL
ZOO
SCHOOL

Ohhhhh!
So THAT'S where you keep all your swords and bazookas.

Yeah. Actually, we DO. Wanna see them?

DUDE. YES.

Let's go!
We need to get these collars out to everyone.
I also really need to grab us some bazookas.
This is the best day of my life!

Abby and I are going to try to find out what's going on with that exterminator.

OH MY GOSH!
AN ABBY AND GOOD BOY TEAM-UP?

Sorry. I'm just REALLY excited.

ME TOO!

So I guess this is where we part ways?

Good luck, dudes! You got this!
You too!

Text me!
You got it!

Let's DO this.

BOOKS!
Let's cut through the park!

AWW, YEAH! SECRET ROUTE!

BEEP
BEEP

Watch where you're going, you hooligans!
Sorry!

Where did you learn to run so fast?

Do you want to know my secret weapon?

Is your secret weapon candy?

MY SECRET WEAPON IS CANDY!

Nice.

Hang on a second.
HUFF
HUFF

I just want to make sure we're going in the right direction.

Uh... Ms. Monica?

Aaron, give me a second, okay?

Aaron...
TAP
TAP

ITCHYYY...

Ms. Monica! Behind you! There are more of 'em!

Okay... Stay back...

SO ITCHY!
ITCH US!
What are we gonna do?

I'll think of something...

Thanks for tagging along with me, Abby!

It's my honor, Mayor Good Boy!

I didn't think I'd be able to help at all...
I've felt kind of useless lately...

I've had this unsure feeling in my stomach for a while...Maybe I just need to eat more?

Speaking of which...You hungry?
My mom packed us some string cheese!

I am ALWAYS down for cheese.

Same.

You don't waste any time, do you?

Abby, there are two types of people in the world. People who take their time peeling their string cheese, and people who just go for it.

I also can't grip that well with these paws...

HA
HA
HA
HA
HA
HA
HA

No, I totally get what you're saying, though. Like my mom always says...

Opposites attract!

CRASH

What was that?

HUFF
HUFF
HUFF

Abby! Wait for me!

Hey!
Get back
here!

NOPE!

CALL
ME
Hey!

GREENWOOD
EXTERMINA
Mayor Good
Boy! I found the
exterminator!

STEP
ON IT!
GREENWOOD
EXTERMINATORS

Did you see that? The mayor and that ratty little know-it-all kid almost spotted me!

So? Who cares what they say?

Who cares? Who cares?

I CARE! STICK TO THE PLAN, OR IT'LL BE THE LAST MISTAKE YOU EVER MAKE!
SHAKE SHAKE
WHAT THE?!

BEEP
BEEP
BEEEEP

There we go. Nice and easy.

Then we get to roll up and pretend to save the day and make that little mutt look like a failure!

There are fleas all over town! Everyone will think it was because they let a DOG become mayor!
Why are you explaining your evil plan again? We've been through this a hundred times!

STOP!

I SAID STOP THE TRUCK!

SCREEEEEEEEECH
GREENWOOD EXTERMINATORS

Well, looks like we found the exterminators again!

Uhh...

Hey! It's YOU!
BORK
BORK
BORK

ABANDON SHIP!

GO GO GO!

Abby!
Wait!

C'mon!
They're getting
away!

Let them go.
At least we know
what's going on
now.
Wait...
do we?

Looks like Old
Man Mervis released
all the fleas himself.
I cannot believe I didn't
think of that! He's worked
at the pest control
company for like one
hundred years!

Abby...
are you okay?

I feel like
I'm forgetting
something?
...

Oh man,
I forgot to text
Ms. Monica!

Wait a second.
Have you seen my
phone?

BUZZ
BUZZ
10 MISSED CALLS
BUZZ

I hope everything is okay...Abby isn't answering!

I'm sure she's fine. Abby is like the last person on earth you ever need to worry about.

It's not your sister that has me worried...

We'll figure that out later.
We gotta start giving these collars to people!

CITY HALL
Looks like we have visitors.

Listen up!
I know this is going to sound weird, but I need everyone to put on one of these dog collars!

CITY HALL

We wanna talk to Mayor Good Boy!
Yeah!
Yeah! I want to pet him!
The mayor is on a very important mission! Trust me.
These are gifts from Mayor Good Boy himself! They'll keep the fleas away!
See! It works on humans too!

Look at this guy. He's covered in fleas. He's disgusting.

No offense.
CLICK

Watch this!

No more fleas!

This gets rid of the fleas?

Aw yeah!

GIVE ME THAT!
NO! ME!
Let's get 'em!

Uh-oh.

BORK!
BORK!
BORK!

Abby!
Mayor Good Boy!

Nice to see everyone!

We're going to help you guys, but you need to help us too!

Put these on. Trust me. I've been using these things since I was a puppy!

SNAP
SNAP
SNAP

I think this is how it's supposed to go on?

Oh, wow. We look so tough now!

Stand still, Edward!

We're going to have to wash all our clothes to get rid of the fleas!

Yes. So everyone get naked. That's an order!

NO, PLEASE DON'T!

We have new clothes inside for everyone. Once you get a collar, please go inside and change.
CITY HALL

A little while later...
You could use one, too.
YES! THIS RULES!
This one might be a little big for you, Aaron.

No way.
This is perfect!

Okay, everybody.
First off, I want to say I love everyone's fashion choices.

HA HA HA HA HA HA HA HA

I don't get it.
SHHH

We're gonna need some help passing out the rest of these collars around town!

We have
a lot of ground to
cover, so let's
split up.

You guys can
take the west side
and south side.

SOUTH
SIIIIIDE!

. . .

Sorry.
I always wanted
to say that but never
had a chance...

And you
guys can cover
the north side and the
east side.

I cannot thank you enough for helping your fellow citizens of Greenwood! You dudes are gonna make me cry!

I also have a special surprise for everyone to help us get back to normal. See you soon! Let's get to work!

I can't believe he won them over that quickly!

He's amazing, isn't he?

We did it!

Abby, did you lose your phone AGAIN?
Don't tell Mom and Dad!
I don't care about your phone... I'm just glad you're okay.
Aww, Aaron...

FAAAAAART

OH MY GOSH GET AWAY FROM ME YOU'RE DISGUSTING!
HA HA HA HA HA HA HA

HA HA HA HA
You should have seen the look on your face!

Yo!

SNIFF
SNIFF

Aaron, dude. You really need to eat more healthy. YIKES!

HA HA HA HA HA HA HA HA HA HA HA HA HA

You guys ready to go?

YEAH!

Let's hand these collars out!

LET'S DO IT!!

READ!

PRODUCE

ADOPT

SHARE
4+4=8
10-6=4
3+3=6
12-6=6

Coffee . . . 1.00
Milk . . . 1.25
Latte . . . 2.00

OMING
OON
BOX OFFICE
COMING
SOON

Later that night...
Wait a second...
You never told me what
happened with the
exterminators!

OH MY GOSH!
I can't believe we forgot
to tell you!

You know
that old guy?
Dad?

Hahaha...no.
The other old guy...
Old Man Mervis!

Oh no!
Did he KILL THE
EXTERMINATORS?

Wait, what? Kill? Aaron, can you just let me finish my story?
Go on.

So anyways... Old Man Mervis IS an exterminator.
Whaaaa?

It was an inside job! Just like in the movies! The exterminators released all the fleas in town!
Wow.

I knew that guy was trouble from the start!

Why would he do that, though?

BECAUSE GREENWOOD DESERVES BETTER!

Yeah, I unleashed the fleas!
I needed to show this town what would REALLY happen if a dog took over.

Got ya.

What's so funny, huh?

I don't know... It's just that I lost my phone earlier...

What are you going on about? Why should I care about your stupid phone?

Well, a good neighbor found my phone and gave it back to me.
AND?

And I just livestreamed you admitting that you released the fleas in town.
The whole town is watching, Mr. Mervis.

What? How? This is entrapment! And what does "livestream" mean?
Is that bad??

SHAKE SHAKE SHAKE
He's back... I knew this would happen...

You need to turn yourself in, Mervis. You can make this easier on yourself.

I ain't doing that! If you want me, you can come and get me!

SEE YA, LOSERS!

Let's go! We can't let him get away again!

Oh man, this is gonna be good!

You think a couple of dumb kids and a mutt are going to stop me? HA!

I'm so sick of this...

OOK
OOK
OOK
...monkey business!

GET OFF ME! GET OFF ME!

WHY DOES THIS KEEP HAPPENING TO ME?

We gotta get that monkey on the payroll!
HA
HA
HA

Oooook?

I guess we're even now.

ARRROOOO
POLICE

WAAAAA

Mr. Mervis? You're under arrest.
POL

YOU'LL PAY FOR THIS, MAYOR GOOD BOY! I'M GONNA GET YOU AND THOSE STUPID KIDS AND THAT MONKEY!
JUST WAIT!

BYE-BYE!

Wow. Guess we should say goodbye to these guys too?

Take a look!

Aww. Bye, fleas!

You guys ready for the surprise?

whisper whisper whisper

Huh?
whisper whisper

Ohhh! Yeah! That's good!

See you in the morning. That's when the real fun begins.

Citizens of Greenwood, are you itching for a little relief from these past couple of days? If you were affected by the recent flea infestation, you won't want to miss this. Come to the Greenwood Park Pool for a special kind of pool party.

-MAYOR GOOD BOY

POOL
Will this itch ever go away?

I'M STILL SO ITCHY!

Thank you for coming, everyone! Trust me, I think you're gonna love what Mayor Good Boy has planned for you!

Aaron, do you copy? The eagle has landed. Over.

Roger. This is Aaron Ableman. We're ready. Over.

We're ready! Bring it in!

Roger that, Aaron. Get ready!
RUMBLE
RUMBLE
OATMEAL

Here goes nothing!
BEEP BEEP

WHOOOSH

Oatmeal!
What's that for?

Special delivery!
When I was a pup and got really itchy, I took an oatmeal bath, and it was the best! I figured, why not all take one together?
I'll try anything to get rid of this itch!
Let's goooooo!
IT WORKS! MAYOR GOOD BOY IS A GENIUS!

. . . .

OATMEAL POOL PARTY!

Woooo!
Cannonball!

Mayor Good Boy rules!
What a great idea!
Dude, don't eat the oatmeal! Gross!

Are you dorks gonna go in the pool or what?
Aaron, don't take this the wrong way, but why are you wearing a suit to the pool?
It's my swimsuit. GET IT?
Aaron, you are eight years old. You are way too young to be making dad jokes.
Yup. Definitely oatmeal.

SHHHH

Huh?

Gotcha!

HA HA HA
HA
BLOOOP

HA
HA
HA
HA
HA
HA
HA
HA

I'm gonna get ya!
HA
HA
HA

Mayor Good Boy...can I ask you a question?

Of course, Abby. What is it?

It's just...

Come on, you
can tell me anything.
That's what friends are
for, right?

I'm just wondering,
like...of all the people
who you could have hired
to help you...

Why did
I pick you
and Aaron?

Yeah...
What's so special about us?

The first time I saw you guys...you have no idea how scared I was that day!
Suddenly, I was in charge of an entire town! I thought I was ready, but...

I still get so scared and nervous... even though I'm supposed to be Mayor Good Boy!

You and your brother didn't even know me and wanted to help! You just jumped in and did the right thing!

The world can really use more people like you and your brother.

Awwww...
squeeeze

I didn't know what would happen, but...

Look around! Everyone is so happy! It wasn't like this a few days ago...I didn't think we could do it, but...

WE did this! Because we worked together!
We make each other stronger!

I think we make a good team.

The town of Greenwood...

The sweetest little place on earth...

Each and every person has a story.

Some have grown up here, and some have just planted their seeds.

But for some, the town has changed.

A once-sleepy community has made national news all because of one little dog.
M. GOOD BOY

PSST. MAYOR GOOD BOY!
M. GOOD BOY

DUDE, WAKE UP!
M. GOOD BOY

Shhhh!

Ahem
ZZZZZ

How did I know he was gonna do this?

Where did I put that...?

CHEESE!
I LOVE CHEESE! WHERE'S
THE CHEESE?

M. GOOD BOY

Ummm...
MUNCH
MUNCH

NOM NOM
NOM

Mayor
Good Boy!
TV reporter!
Remember?

Uhh...
M. GOOD BOY

Hi!
Hey! Hello,
Greenwood!

Don't laugh.
Don't laugh.
Don't laugh.

I have to say, Mayor Good Boy, you always know how to make an entrance!

Thank you, Steenz. Hope it wasn't too... CHEESY!

M GOOD BOY
No, no, no, no...

Ha ha ha!
Oh, stop. You're cute AND funny!

So tell me, Mayor Good Boy, how do you do it? Being mayor seems like a really tough job!

Great question, Steenz. The truth is that Greenwood is full of great people!

People like my friends Abby and Aaron and Ms. Monica here!

C'mon, dudes.
Don't be shy!
GREENW

Hello
again!

Hey!
I remember
you guys!

That's right!
My name is Abby
Ableman!

Official
junior aide to
Mayor Good
Boy!
OFFICIAL JUNIOR AIDE

What's up, Greenwood! It's your boy Aaron Ableman, and we're here LIVE!

HI, MOM! HI, DAD!

Wow! I can't believe I'm on live TV!

Aaron! Come here.

And who might you be?

Hi! I'm Ms. Monica! I work for Mayor Good Boy!

It's so great to meet you! I have a question for the little ones here...

Can you share any advice for kids out there who want to help their community?

I recommend eating around one hundred boogers a day and smelling at least five hundred farts a week.

UHHH, YEAH! Of course we have advice!
HA
HA
HA

Just because you're a kid doesn't mean you can't change the world!

Wow, Abby. You sound like you have it all figured out!

Like, look at my little brother. He's literally the grossest person I've ever met. One time he ate a hot dog that fell into the pool!

It was only underwater for a few minutes! What's the big deal?

If Aaron can help someone, so can you!
It's true!

If you'll excuse me...we have something to do...

So what's next for Mayor Good Boy?

I have one more important thing to do...

I'm going to hang out with my friends!

PIZZA

HOW to DRAW MAYOR GOOD BOY

① Draw a circle.

② Now draw two more circles!

③ Add two triangles and a backward "C."

④ Add 5 sticks. (These will be the legs.)

⑤ Make those sticks into feet! (See?)

⑥ Add his face and nose!

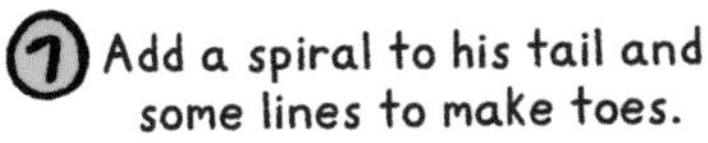

7 Add a spiral to his tail and some lines to make toes.

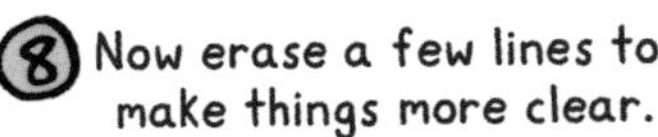

8 Now erase a few lines to make things more clear.

9 Add details! Fluff! Collar! His tongue!

10 Don't forget to add color!

And there you have it.
Look at Mayor Good Boy go!

HOW to DRAW Aaron Ableman!

① Draw a bean.

② Add a long tube for his torso.

③ Add four lines attached to the tube.

④ Add feet to the lines! They're his legs!

⑤ Add two arms.

⑥ Now add two hands!

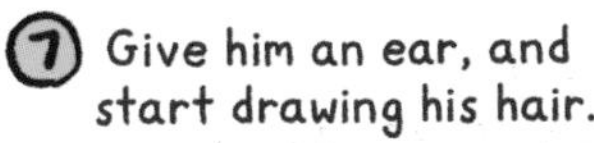

7. Give him an ear, and start drawing his hair.

8. Add more hair.

9. Add even more hair!

10. Add two circles for eyes.

11. Add Aaron's face and shoelaces.

12. Add color, and you're done! That's Aaron!

HOW to DRAW Abby Ableman

1. Draw a circle. That's Abby's head!

2. Add a cone under the circle.

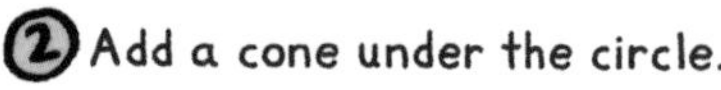

3. Add three lines under the cone.

4. Draw her skirt, and turn the lines into legs!

5. Add two arms.

6. Add two hands.

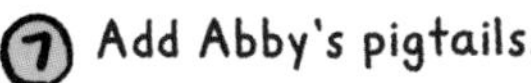

7 Add Abby's pigtails.

8 Add two circles for her glasses.

9 Now we'll add some details: her face, eyes, and glasses.

10 Add the top part of Abby's hair here.

11 Then there's the last details: her ears, bow, jacket, and boots!

12 Just add color, and you're done!

I will use my bark more than my bite.

I will try to fart less than a hundred times a week.

I will use my voice to speak for the voiceless.

I will help make my community a better place, one day at a time.

I will never give up, even when times are hard.

I will remember that being different is what makes me special.

I will remember that positive change takes time,
but it's worth fighting for.

I will always root for the underdog.

Hi! We're going to show you HOW TO CONTACT YOUR REPRESENTATIVES!

In a democracy, a community elects their own representatives.
But even if you're too young to vote, you can still talk to them about your concerns!

It is their job to listen to you and your neighbors. So make your voice heard!

STEP #1:
Think about something you could do to help your community.
LET'S FILL THE PUBLIC POOL WITH SNAKES!

NO, AARON! I mean like how the Greenwood community garden needs more funding!
Aw.

STEP #2:
Find your representatives' contact information on the internet. You can look for your local elected officials, such as city council members.
If you want to talk about a wider issue, you can find officials on a state or national level, like your senators!

AND STEP #3:
Write them a letter.
Send them an email.
Or call them on the phone!

When reaching out, remember to personalize your message and be specific. Try to focus on one or two issues at a time!
Ask an adult if you need help finding information or writing a letter!
I still think we should fill the pool with snakes.

DAVE SCHEIDT is a writer from Chicago. When he's not writing comic books, he likes watching monster movies and eating snacks. He first started writing stories when he was ten years old and hasn't stopped since.

davescheidt.com

DAVE THANKS

I would first like to thank my family for all the years of support. My father, Thomas Scheidt, who was literally the first person on earth to read my stories and sacrificed everything to help me find my voice. My late mother, Elizabeth Scheidt, was one of the toughest people I have ever met. She had so much love to give even at the very end, and I miss her every day. To my brother, Eric, who filled my life with comic books and toys that shaped me and who supported my creativity since the very beginning. To my sister, Sarah, who has been with me during my darkest days and never gave up on me and made sure I turned out okay. I love you all deeply, and without you this book wouldn't exist.

I would also like to thank Natalie Djordjevic for always believing in me and for the thankless work you have done for my career. I would be lost without you, and I'm so glad to have you in my life. The amount of love and wisdom and laughs you bring is immeasurable. Love you forever and ever.

Thank you to everyone at Random House (Whitney, Gina, Patrick, Nicole) who believed in our little doggie and saw that his story was worth telling. I'd also like to thank Charlie Olsen, Scoot McMahon, Yehudi Mercado, Whitney Gardener, Joey Weiser, Kayla Miller, Steenz and Keya, Ryan, Carrie and Kirby Browne, Josephine M. Yales, Patrick Brower, Nick and Selene Idell, Art Baltazar, Franco Aureliani, Mitch Gerards, Jess Smart Smiley, Kenny Porter, Kris Erickson, Alejandro Rosado, John and Aneta Baran, Tim Beard, Tara Kurtzhals, Tara O'Connor, Andrea Colvin, Hazel Newlevant, Brandon Snider, Trevor Henderson, James Zespy, Shawna Gore, Eric Roesner, Raphael Espinoza, Mike Costa, Andrew Rostan, Rachel Roberts, Bethany Bryan, Elizabeth Brei, Brian Level, Andy Eschenbach, Liz Kozik, Steve Seeley, Jenny Frison, Brian Crowley, Sean Dove, Tony Blando, Jen Sabella, Robert Wilson IV, Tini Howard, Elio, Christopher Sebela, RJ Casey, and everyone and anyone who has supported me throughout the years.

I'd also like to thank each and every librarian, educator, and bookseller who is out there helping kids find themselves in the pages of a book. You are so important, and I'm so grateful to work in an industry with great people like you.

Last but not least, I would like to send all my love to Miranda Harmon. Without her incredibly sweet and beautiful cartooning, this book wouldn't exist. She has brought this book to life in a way I could have never imagined. I am in awe of her creativity, talent, and hard work, and it's been an honor creating this world with her.

MIRANDA HARMON grew up in Florida and now lives in Los Angeles, where she works and takes care of several houseplants. She graduated from Goucher College and studied comics at the Sequential Artists Workshop. Even though she grew up with cats, she loves dogs too.

@MirandaMHarmon
mirandaharmon.com

MIRANDA THANKS

First of all, I'd like to thank my parents for being so supportive from the other side of the country. I love and miss you both. Thank you to Tom Hart, Leela Corman, and everyone else at the Sequential Artists Workshop in Gainesville, Florida, for their guidance and kindness. I might not be making books now if I hadn't been given use of the SAW Risograph machine for two years. To my comics friends, you all have changed the course of my life for the better. Thank you for all the convention memories and for helping me navigate this world. Thank you to my agent, Charlie, and to Dave, Whitney, Gina, Patrick, and everyone at Random House for helping this book become something very special. I feel lucky to be a part of this team. Thank you, Reed and Sarah, for your help flatting the book. And thank you to Eric for helping me stay grounded when things get shaky. I love you very much.

ABBY + AARON

Behind the SKETCH!

DON'T MISS A SINGLE

MAYOR GOOD BOY

ADVENTURE!

MAYOR GOOD BOY
GOES HOLLYWOOD
Dave Scheidt
COMING IN 2022
MAYOR GOOD BOY
TURNS BAD
Dave Scheidt
Miranda Harmon
Coming in 2023